Friendly

A Cherrytree Book

Designed and produced by
A S Publishing

First published 1993
by Cherrytree Press Ltd
Windsor Bridge Road
Bath, Avon BA2 3AX

Reprinted 1995

British Library Cataloguing in Publication Data
Amos, Janine
  Friendly. – (Feelings Series)
  I. Title II. Green, Gwen III. Series
  152.4

ISBN 0-7451-5196-5

Printed and bound in Spain by Graficas Reunidas, S.A.

Friendly

By Janine Amos

Illustrated by Gwen Green

CHERRYTREE BOOKS

Zahid's story

David and Zahid had been to swimming club. Zahid was hungry. He was thinking about his dinner. It might be baked beans and sausages. That was his favourite. Just then David stopped.

"Hurry up," said Zahid.

"I've lost my watch," said David.

Zahid groaned, "We can't go back now – it's too far. And we're nearly home."

David didn't move. "That watch cost a lot of money. I can't go home without it. My mum'll kill me!" said David.

Zahid laughed. "Don't be daft!" he said. But he thought that David's mum might shout. She did get pretty cross sometimes.

"Hold on! I may have put my watch in here," said David. He threw down his duffle bag. Zahid watched his friend take everything out of the bag. Soon David's trunks, his soap and his wet towel were lying on the pavement. A dog sniffed at them.

"Let's try your bag," said David. So Zahid shook his towel, trunks and soap on to the pavement too. They found some crisps in the bag. But there was no watch.

"Have you checked your pockets?" asked Zahid.

David checked them all – twice.

"It's no good," he sighed. "It's lost."

How do you think David feels?

It was windy. Zahid started to feel cold. He thought again about his dinner. David was packing his duffle bag very slowly. Zahid jumped up and down to keep warm.

"Your mum will 'phone the pool straightaway," said Zahid. "Your watch will be safe."

"I don't want to go home without it," David said again. He looked really worried.

What could Zahid do to help?

Zahid had an idea.

"I know," said Zahid. "I'll come home with you. It's better with two. And your mum won't be so cross if you've got a friend with you."

"Great!" said David.

The two boys ran all the way to David's house.

How is David feeling now?
How do you think Zahid is feeling?

David's mum was in the kitchen.

"Hello, you two!" she said as the boys walked in.

"She doesn't look at all cross," thought Zahid. But you could never be sure with David's mum.

"Hi, Mum," said David in a quiet voice. He was glad that Zahid was standing next to him.

"Here goes!" thought Zahid.

Just then David ran to the table. He could see
something lying there. It was something belonging to him.
It was his watch! Quickly, David picked it up.

"You forgot to wear your watch this morning," said
David's mum. "It's just as well – you might have lost it at
the pool."

David gave Zahid a huge grin.

"Could Zahid stay to dinner, Mum?" asked David.

"I should think so," smiled David's mum. She turned
to Zahid.

"Do you like sausages?" she asked.

Feeling like Zahid

Zahid was cold and hungry. He wanted to go home for his dinner. But he stayed to help David instead. Have you ever been friendly like Zahid?

Someone else

Being friendly means thinking about someone else. Pretend to be them – just for a minute. Think how they might be feeling. Is there anything you can do to help?

Friends

Friends can share a
problem. They can't make
the problem go away. But
they can talk about it – and
make the problem seem
smaller. Sometimes friends
can help just by being
around.

Think about it

Read the stories in this
book. Think about the
people in them. Do you feel
like them sometimes? Think
how people have been
friendly to you. How can
you be friendly to others?

Rachael's story

Rachael was having a party. She was keeping it a secret. Only Rachael's best friend Jane knew. They were making the party invitations together. "It will be a secret party – until the invitations are ready!" laughed Rachael.

But Jane didn't keep the secret. She told Anna. And soon the whole class knew.

"You've spoilt my surprise," wailed Rachael.

"I didn't mean to," said Jane, looking down.

"You promised not to tell," Rachael said. "I always keep your secrets."

Jane went red. "I'm sorry," she said.

Rachael was cross. "I don't like you any more!" she shouted.

After school, Rachael ran right past Jane. She joined up with some other girls.

"Hey! Wait for me!" Jane called.

"I'm not talking to you!" shouted Rachael. "And you're not coming to my party!"

"I don't want to come to your stupid party!" shouted Jane. But she didn't look happy. She looked as if she might cry. Rachael was pleased.

Why do you think Rachael was pleased?
How do you think Jane feels?

When Rachael got home she slammed the door behind her. Her mum was reading a newspaper.

"I'm fed up with Jane," said Rachael. She told her mum what had happened.

"Jane's not coming to my party," said Rachael. "And I'm not talking to her ever again."

"Mm," said Rachael's mum. "Jane shouldn't have broken her promise. But she's your best friend. Can't you forgive her?"

"No!" said Rachael.

Do you think Rachael should forgive Jane?

Later Rachael got out the party invitations. They were nearly ready. Rachael finished the colouring. She started to fill in the names. It wasn't so much fun making them without Jane. Rachael found Jane's invitation and scribbled on it with a black felt-tip.

Rachael looked at the spoilt invitation. She felt sad. She remembered Jane calling her party 'stupid'. But that didn't make Rachael feel any better. "I do wish Jane hadn't told," Rachael thought. "I wish she was still my friend."

Rachael's mum sat down next to her. "Cheer up, Rachael," she said.

"Who's your best friend, Mum?" Rachael asked.

"Your dad, I suppose," said Rachael's mum. "And Aunty Pauline."

"I bet Aunty Pauline doesn't break her promises," said Rachael.

"She does sometimes," said Rachael's mum. She looked a bit cross. "In fact Aunty Pauline promised to come over to help me with your party. But today she telephoned me. She's going on holiday instead."

Rachael put down her felt-tip. She looked at her mum.

"Will you forgive her?" Rachael asked. She liked Aunty Pauline.

"Yes," replied Rachael's mum. "Pauline and I have some good times together." Rachael's mum smiled. "Sometimes our friends do things we don't like. We get cross with them – but they're still our friends."

Is Rachael's mum right?

At bedtime Rachael was still busy.

"Come along, Rachael," said her mum. "What are you doing?"

"I'm making another invitation," said Rachael, yawning. "It's for Jane."

"I thought you weren't friendly with Jane any more?" said Rachael's mum.

"I'm forgiving her," said Rachael.

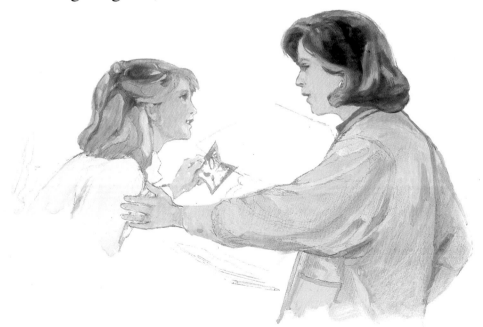

Why has Rachael changed her mind?

Feeling like Rachael

Have you ever felt like Rachael? Has anyone ever made you so cross that you shouted, "I don't like you"? Perhaps you didn't really mean it. You just meant that you didn't like what they'd done.

Talking about it

Sometimes our friends upset us. They hurt us by the things they say or do. They've forgotten to think about our feelings. Then we have to remind them. We have to talk about it. We have to tell them how we feel – or they won't know. There's no need to stop being friends.

21

Adam's story

The group of boys stood in the playground. Tom had a plan.

"Let's go to the park after school," he said. "We can try that new tactic!"

"I'll be trainer!" shouted Steve.

Adam was pleased. They could use his new football. He gave it a bounce.

Adam saw someone watching them. It was the new boy in the class. He was standing on his own in the playground. Adam wondered if the new boy wanted to play. But Tom was already racing away.

"Hurry up!" called Tom.

Adam didn't want to be left behind.

"See you!" he waved to the new boy. Adam ran off after his friends.

After the game Adam went home for tea. Adam's dad and his big brother Jason were there.

"I saved a goal," said Adam.

"Who did you play with?" asked Adam's dad.

"Tom and Steve and the others," answered Adam. Then he told his dad about the new boy at school.

"Did he go to the park with you?" asked Adam's dad.

"No," said Adam.

"I bet he felt left out," said Jason.

"Tom didn't ask him to come," Adam said.

"Who cares?" said Jason. "You could have asked him."

Is Jason right?

Jason put down his comic.

"You were only a baby when we moved here," he told Adam. "You don't remember being new. But I do. I didn't know anyone. It was horrible."

"But you've got lots of friends!" said Adam.

"I have now," said Jason.

Adam was interested. "How did you make friends?" he asked.

"I took my comic collection into school," said Jason. "I was reading it on my own. One boy asked if he could have a look. Then some of his friends came over. There was a big group. Soon I knew lots of boys."

Adam thought for a while.

"But why didn't you go over to the boys?" he asked his brother. "Why did you have to wait?"

"It was hard to do that," said Jason. "Those boys all knew each other. I was the odd one out."

"I know what Jason means," said Adam's dad. "I remember being new here too. It took me a long time to make friends."

"What happened?" asked Adam and Jason together.

"I remember feeling lonely," said Adam's dad, "especially at lunchtimes. I sat on my own eating my sandwiches. I did the crossword."

"And what happened then?" asked Adam.

"One day someone asked me to the canteen. I met lots of other people. Now I go there every lunchtime." Adam's dad laughed, "That's why I'm so fat!"

"Being new sounds awful!" said Adam. "I'll ask the new boy to play football tomorrow."

"That would be a friendly thing to do," said Adam's dad.

The next day at school Adam ran up to his friends. He couldn't wait to join in the game. Then Adam remembered the new boy.

"Hi!" he called. "I'm Adam."

"I'm John," the new boy called back. And Adam kicked him the ball.

After the game the boys crowded round John. They wanted to know all about him. They had lots of questions to ask.

Adam looked at John and the rest of the group. "It's a bit like my brother's story," he thought.

How did Jason's story help?

Making friends

It's hard to be friendly if you're new. Everyone else knows each other. You feel all alone. So what Adam did was important. He helped John to be part of the group.

Friends' welcome

Have you ever been friendly, like Adam? Have you ever welcomed a new boy or girl into the group? If you have, you'll know that it's a good feeling. It's a very good feeling to be welcomed too!

Needing a friend

We all need a friend sometimes. And there's always someone else who needs a friend. Are you good at being friendly? Who's been friendly to you?

Being a friend

Think about the stories in this book. Zahid, Rachael and Adam each learned different things about friendship. What have you learned? How many ways can you show that you're a good friend?

If you are feeling frightened or unhappy, don't keep it to yourself. Talk to an adult you can trust, like a parent or a teacher. If you feel really alone, you could telephone or write to one of these offices. Remember, there is always someone who can help.

Childline
Freephone 0800 1111
Address: Freepost 1111, London N1 0BR

Childline for children in care
Freephone 0800 884444 (6 – 10pm)

NSPCC Child Protection Line
Freephone 0800 800500

The Samaritans
Dial 100 – The operator will put you through.